I'm Big Enough

Cos H. Davis, Jr.
Illustrated by Michael Sloan

Broadman Press
Nashville, Tennessee

© Copyright 1990 . Broadman Press
All rights reseved
4243-42
ISBN: 0-8054-4342-8
Dewey Decimal Classification: C264.36
Subject Heading: BAPTISM // LORD'S SUPPER
Library of Congress Catalog Card Number: 89-24027
Printed in the United States of America

Library of Congress Cataloging-in-Publication Data
Davis, Cos,H.
    I'm big enough.
    Summary: A simple introduction to the ordinances of
baptism and the Lord's Supper.
    1. Sacraments—Baptists—Juvenile literature.
2. Baptists—Membership—Juvenile literature. 3. Southern
Baptist Convention—Membership—Juvenile literature.
[1. Baptism. 2. Lord's Supper. 3 Baptists] I. Sloan,
Mike, ill. II. Title.
BX6338.D38   1990   234'.161   89-24027
ISBN 0-8054-4342-8

Hello. My name is Matthew. My family calls me Matt. I'm six years old. I'm in the first grade.

I'm big enough to do lots of things. I can brush my teeth and comb my hair.

I pick up my toys and help keep my room clean. Mom says I'm big enough to help do many things.

Best of all I can ride my bike without training wheels.

I live with my dad and mom. I have a sister Kim. Kim is ten. Our dog's name is Champ.

Supper at my house is a special time. Mom fixes good food, and we talk about things we did during the day. Kim and I ask questions about things we don't understand. Mom and Dad try to answer our questions. It's fun being part of my family!

Before bedtime Mom or Dad reads to us from the Bible or tells a Bible story. Sometimes we talk about things we learn at church. Other times we sing a favorite song we learned at church. Mom and Dad say it's important to know about God. That's why we read the Bible.

I usually think of lots of questions before I go to sleep at night. I like to ask questions like, "Where do butterflies come from?" Sometimes I ask questions about God and church. Mom says most children like to ask questions. She also says that asking questions is a good way to learn.

4

Dad and Mom take Kim and me to church. They say I'm big enough to be still and understand some of the worship service. I sing from the songbook. If I do not understand something about the service, I ask about it. I whisper so I will not disturb others who are trying to worship.

Sometimes I wait and ask my question on the way home. I have lots of questions about God and things that happen at church. I am sure glad I have a Mom and Dad who try to help me.

I am growing, and I understand more about God and His world everyday. Sometimes it does not seem fair that I cannot do things bigger people do. I feel left out--like a little kid.

My sister, Kim, gets to do things I do not get to do. But I think I'm big enough to do some of the things she does.

This summer Kim was baptized. Mom and Dad were happy. They said it was a very special day for Kim and our family. I sat on Dad's lap during the worship service so I could see what was happening.

Kim was dressed in a white robe. When it was her turn to be baptized, she walked down into the water in the baptistry. The pastor was standing there. Then he said some words and pushed her under the water. She was soaking wet when she came up, but she looked happy. We were all happy.

8

After Kim was baptized, I thought I should be baptized too. I said to Mom, "I want to be baptized like Kim was. I think I'm big enough."

Mom did not seem too surprised. She said, "Yes, Matt, you are getting bigger each day. Tell me why you want to be baptized." I told her I wanted to please her and Dad and God. She hugged me and told me we would talk more when Dad came home.

When Dad came home, he and Mom talked to me before I went to sleep. Dad said, "Matt, your Mom told me you have been asking questions about being baptized. We're glad you are asking questions. Let's talk about baptism when we have our family time tomorrow night. Is that OK?"

I told them that would be good. They hugged me good night. I was happy, and soon I was asleep.

The next day while I played, I wondered what it would be like to be baptized. Sometimes it seems scary. I don't swim very well yet, and I guess I'm a little afraid of the water. Why are people baptized? How old do you have to be to be baptized? Will you go to heaven if you're not baptized?

That evening at our family time, we talked about our church. We talked about what we like about our church. Dad asked Kim to tell us what it was like to be baptized. She said that after she accepted Jesus as her Savior, she wanted to be baptized. That's what Jesus had said to do. She also wanted others to know she was a Christian by seeing her baptized. I had not thought about those reasons. She laughed and said she was scared and nervous when she went down into the water to be baptized.

Dad laughed. He said he knew what Kim meant. He said he was older than Kim when he accepted Jesus. He was about twenty-one, but he was a little nervous too.

Then I said, "Dad, I did not think you were ever afraid of anything."

Dad said, "I guess I was more excited than afraid. Being baptized was a way of saying to the people who watched that I had accepted Jesus as my Savior and turned my life over to Him. I was doing something very important!"

Mom surprised us all. "I have a picture of when I was baptized," she said. "I was just a couple of years older than Kim. I was excited the day I went forward in our church and told the pastor I wanted Jesus as my Savior. He talked with me, and I was baptized the next Sunday. Our church did not have a baptistry, so guess where I was baptized? I was baptized in the river after church the next Sunday morning."

I enjoyed hearing my family tell about being baptized. Dad said, "Matt, you have heard us tell about being baptized. What did each of us do? What kind of decision did we make before being baptized?"

"You wanted Jesus to be your Savior?" I asked.

"Yes, Matt," Dad said. "Baptism comes after a person accepts Jesus as his Savior. Baptism is a way of telling others you have asked Jesus to forgive your sins."

"Does being baptized wash away your sins? Is it like taking a bath and having your sins washed away?" I asked.

"Matt," Mom said, "you take a bath at home to wash the dirt off your body. I can understand how you might think baptism washes your sins away. But sin is inside us, and water cannot wash that away. When we ask Jesus to be

our Savior, He forgives our sins.
Baptism means you have trusted Jesus
to forgive your sins and to help you live
as He wants you to live."

"Then, when can I be baptized? I love Jesus."

"Of course you do," Mom said. "You can be baptized when God helps you know you need to let Him come into your life and forgive your sins. God will help you know when to accept Jesus as your Savior. When you have made that decision, you can be baptized." Mom hugged me. "As you continue to grow, God will help you understand."

I thought about the things my family had said about being baptized. I understood some of the words my parents had used. I had heard our preacher talk about them. But I did not understand yet about God telling me I need Jesus as my Savior. I am growing and getting bigger every day, but I don't think I'm ready to be baptized. It is OK if I wait until I understand more.

The next morning at breakfast I told my family that I wanted to wait for a while to be baptized. Kim said she was proud of me for waiting. Dad told me I was really growing to be able to wait until I want to be baptized for the right reason. I was happy about my decision. Mom made blueberry pancakes for breakfast--my favorite!

Mom said, "Matt, keep asking questions, and we'll talk anytime you need to talk. God will help you know when you need to make your decision. That day will come before you know it. Then you can be baptized."

The next Sunday we went to church. Mom and Dad told me we would be having the Lord's Supper at church that morning. "Why don't we call it the Lord's Lunch instead of the Lord's Supper?" I thought.

The preacher said some things about the Lord's Supper. He used a word I had not heard before. *Ordinance* was the word he used. He told us that only those who had trusted Jesus as their Savior could take the Lord's Supper.

REMEMBRANCE OF ME

This was not a real supper at all like I have at home. It was not even a real lunch. Do you know what was served at this supper? Well, it was not hot dogs or hamburgers. People who ate the supper had two things. They had a tiny piece of bread or cracker and a tiny glass of grape juice. Everybody would need to eat lunch when they got home.

I noticed other things about this supper. We did not go to the table where the food was. The food was brought to us. And only one thing was served at a time. The piece of bread was served first. Then the pastor used some words of Jesus from the Bible: "This is my body." Then everyone ate the bread. Was this really Jesus' body? It looked like a piece of cracker to me. It smelled like cracker. I smelled the piece Dad was holding before he ate it.

Everyone finished eating the bread. Another tray was passed. This time everyone took a small glass of juice. They waited until the preacher said some more words Jesus used: "This is my blood," and everyone drank the juice. I do not know why the preacher called it blood. Anyone could see it was grape juice. After this we sang a song and went home.

I decided I liked the Lord's Supper at our church. There was something special about it. Everyone was very quiet. They were quieter than I have ever seen them before. I did not understand much about what all of this meant. I had my questions ready for Mom and Dad on the way home.

Mom and Dad were not surprised that I had questions. "Why can't I take the Lord's Supper with the rest of you?"

Mom said, "I know you must feel left out of something very special, but why do you think you cannot take the supper yet?"

I told her I heard the preacher say the supper was for people who had accepted Jesus as their Savior.

"That is right," Mom said. "The supper is for people who have accepted Jesus. Someday God will help you know when you need to accept Him."

Dad asked me if I had heard the pastor use the word *ordinance*. I nodded yes. "Do you know what the word means?" he asked.

"No," I said, "what does it mean?"

He told me an ordinance is something special for the church to do. It shows us what Jesus has done to save people. Our church has two ordinances. They are baptism and the Lord's Supper. When a person is baptized and takes the Lord's Supper, it means he has accepted Jesus as his Savior.

As we ate lunch, I thought of something else I did not understand. "That wasn't really Jesus' blood and body, was it?"

Kim said, "No, Matt, that was a cracker and juice."

"Then why did the preacher say it was Jesus' body and blood?" I asked.

"Because the cracker is to remind us that Jesus gave His body and died for us on the cross. And the juice is to remind us that He bled for us when He died on to the cross," Dad said.

I'm growing bigger every day. Someday God will help me know when I need to accept Jesus as my Savior. Then I will be ready to be baptized and take the Lord's Supper too!

I'm glad my parents help me understand things I need to know. I like my family. I like being me. I'm big enough to do many things.